HATSHEPSUT
HIS MAJESTY, HERSELF

BY CATHERINE M. ANDRONIK
ILLUSTRATED BY JOSEPH DANIEL FIEDLER

ATHENEUM BOOKS FOR YOUNG READERS
NEW YORK ◆ LONDON ◆ TORONTO ◆ SYDNEY ◆ SINGAPORE

Atheneum Books for Young Readers
An imprint of Simon & Schuster Children's Publishing Division
1230 Avenue of the Americas, New York, New York 10020

Book design by David A. Caplan
The text of this book is set in Centaur.
The illustrations in this book are rendered in alkyd on paper.
Printed in Hong Kong

2 4 6 8 10 9 7 5 3 1

Library of Congress Cataloging-in-Publication Data
Andronik, Catherine M.
Hatshepsut, his majesty, herself / by Catherine M. Andronik ;
illustrated by Joseph Daniel Fiedler.—1st ed.   p. cm.
Summary: A picture book biography of Hatshepsut, a queen in ancient Egypt
who declared herself king and ruled as such for more than twenty years.
Includes bibliographical references.
ISBN 0-689-82562-5
1. Hatshepsut, Queen of Egypt—Juvenile literature. 2. Queens—Egypt—
Biography—Juvenile literature. 3. Pharaohs—Biography—Juvenile literature.
[1. Hatshepsut, Queen of Egypt. 2. Kings, queens, rulers, etc. 3. Egypt—
Civilization—To 332 B. C.] I. Fiedler, Joseph Daniel, ill. II. Title.
DT87.15 .A53 2000   932'.014'092—dc21   [B] 98-52675

FIRST
EDITION

FOR FRANK
— C.A.

TO PINGTING
— J.F.

A TIMELINE OF HATSHEPSUT'S EGYPT

The years of each pharaoh's reign are only approximate. In ancient Egypt, when a new king came to the throne, it was Year I—and when the next pharaoh succeeded him, it was Year I again. Archaeologists have tried to find a correspondence between the ancient Egyptian way of numbering years and our way, but there are discrepancies and disagreements. Hatshepsut ruled approximately between the years 1479 B.C. and 1458 B.C.

Because hieroglyphics do not always correspond to modern letters, there is also disagreement about the spelling of ancient Egyptian names. For example, some authors spell Hatshepsut as "Hatchepsut" or "Hatshepsuit." Tuthmosis is the Greek version of "Thutmose." "Senenmut" is sometimes spelled "Senmut." I've chosen one spelling for each name and have tried to be consistent.

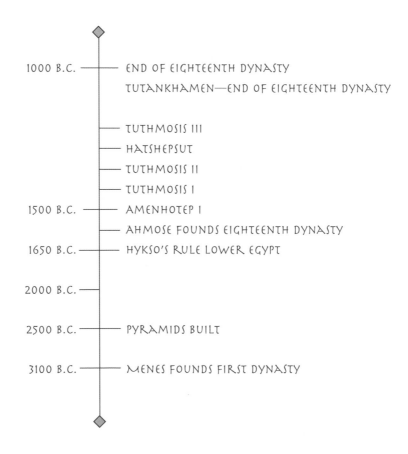

1000 B.C.	END OF EIGHTEENTH DYNASTY
	TUTANKHAMEN—END OF EIGHTEENTH DYNASTY
	TUTHMOSIS III
	HATSHEPSUT
	TUTHMOSIS II
	TUTHMOSIS I
1500 B.C.	AMENHOTEP I
	AHMOSE FOUNDS EIGHTEENTH DYNASTY
1650 B.C.	HYKSO'S RULE LOWER EGYPT
2000 B.C.	
2500 B.C.	PYRAMIDS BUILT
3100 B.C.	MENES FOUNDS FIRST DYNASTY

"NEVER WAS DONE THE LIKE SINCE THE BEGINNING."

A splendid temple is set into the cliffs at Deir el-Bahri (DARE el-BAH-ree), Egypt, near the modern-day city of Luxor, which in ancient times was called Thebes. The temple was dedicated to the god Amen (AH-men), but it also served as a pharaoh's mortuary temple—the place where the king's soul, or *ka*, would live after the king had died, where family and friends could visit a statue of their loved one and leave gifts. The walls of the temple are carved and painted with scenes from the life of this pharaoh: a birth overseen by gods, a triumphant coronation, the excitement of the return of an expedition to an exotic land. In the years since this pharaoh's time, vandals have defaced some of the pictures, and the royal name on the inscriptions has been erased and carved over. But the identity of the king who created this beautiful temple, and who lived the life pictured on its walls, is known in spite of the mutilations. The pharaoh's name is Hatshepsut. Hatshepsut's claim to fame—and the most likely motive behind the vandalism—is that she was ancient Egypt's only successful female king.

"HER MAJESTY WAS A MAIDEN."

As a little girl, Hatshepsut lived a comfortable, even pampered, life. Her father was Pharaoh Tuthmosis (tooth-MOE-sis), the rich, powerful, respected, and beloved king of Egypt, and her mother was Queen Ahmose. Besides a sister named Neferubity, Hatshepsut had half brothers named Tuthmosis, Wadjmose, and Amenmose, all sons of women in her father's harem. They may not have been fully royal, as she was, but because they were boys, they rather than Hatshepsut were being trained to succeed their father as pharaoh.

Hatshepsut was a bright and curious child. Her father, the pharaoh, may have encouraged her curiosity. He took her with him on one of his journeys across his vast desert land and showed her the marvels built by other pharaohs centuries earlier: huge pyramid tombs, towering statues, awe-inspiring temples to Egypt's many gods. Maybe Tuthmosis even included his young daughter in activities usually reserved for men and boys, like hunting crocodiles along the banks of the Nile. Perhaps Hatshepsut would have been more comfortable hunting in a boy's kilt than in the long, narrow dresses worn by women of her time.

But Tuthmosis was not intentionally raising Hatshepsut as if she were another son or a future king, and even an occasional crocodile hunt would be out of the question once she was grown. She was being prepared for a life as a queen, the royal wife of a pharaoh. She learned to read and write, to manage the household help, to make herself beautiful despite the prominent nose she'd inherited from her father's side of the family, and to take part in the many religious rituals a pharaoh and his queen had to conduct to preserve *maat*—ancient Egypt's sense of cosmic order.

"I MADE EGYPT THE SUPERIOR OF EVERY LAND."

Hatshepsut came from an ancestral line, or dynasty, of strong and effective leaders devoted to the welfare of Egypt. Hers was the eighteenth dynasty to rule Egypt since Menes became the country's first pharaoh around 3100 B.C. and founded the First Dynasty.

Around 1600 B.C., invaders from Asia called the Hyksos (HICK-sos) gained control of northern Egypt, dividing the country in two. The ruler of southern Egypt, Sekenenre Tao (seck-en-EN-ray TOW) II, died in his attempt to drive the Hyksos out of the country. But his son Ahmose continued his father's mission and finally succeeded in expelling the invaders. When he became pharaoh and reunited his divided country, Ahmose received Egypt's "double crown": white for the south (Upper Egypt), and red for the north (Lower Egypt). Several generations later, in Hatshepsut's time, any mention of the hated Hyksos still stirred up strong patriotic feeling among the Egyptians.

King Ahmose's son Amenhotep (ah-men-HOE-tep) had no male heir, so he chose a respected warrior, Tuthmosis, to become pharaoh after him. Tuthmosis I proved himself a mighty conqueror. In the course of his reign he defeated Nubia, Egypt's enemy to the south. Then he led Egypt's armies northeast, all the way to Syria and the Euphrates (yoo-FRAY-tees) River. He also added to the great temple complex at Karnak, not far from Thebes.

To make his claim to the throne more legitimate, Tuthmosis took Ahmose, a close relative of Pharaoh Amenhotep, as his Great Wife. Some say Queen Ahmose was

Amenhotep's daughter; others, his sister. Like many of the queens of this dynasty, Queen Ahmose had a reputation for being strong-willed and wise. She was also powerful, for much of the responsibility for continuing the dynasty was hers. One of the queen's many titles was "God's Wife," since Egyptians thought of the pharaoh as the incarnation of the gods Re (RAY) and Horus (HAW-russ). Any child the God's Wife bore would be divine, and therefore royal.

Hatshepsut, royal daughter of Pharaoh Tuthmosis and his Great Wife Ahmose, grew up in an Egypt that was peaceful, prosperous, and respected throughout the known world.

Despite this prosperity, all but one of Hatshepsut's siblings died. Fatal diseases were common, deadly creatures such as scorpions flourished in the Egyptian desert, accidents happened, and a doctor's treatment was often more superstitious than scientific. When the time came for Pharaoh Tuthmosis to name an heir to his throne, only one son remained: Tuthmosis, son of Mutnofret, a woman of the pharaoh's harem. When he became pharaoh, young Tuthmosis would have little choice but to marry a woman of the royal blood. Marriages between close relatives were customary within ancient Egypt's royal family, so Hatshepsut was destined to become her half brother's wife. As the sole child of the pharaoh and the God's Wife, Hatshepsut was her dynasty's last hope to keep the royal bloodlines of Egypt intact.

"THE KING RESTED FROM LIFE, GOING FORTH TO HEAVEN, HAVING COMPLETED HIS YEARS IN GLADNESS OF HEART."

Hatshepsut's father, Pharaoh Tuthmosis I, died at the relatively old age of fifty. His secret tomb, the first underground chamber to be hidden in the towering cliffs of the Valley of the Kings, just northwest of Thebes, had been excavated years in advance. The fine sarcophagus (sar-KOFF-ah-guss), or stone coffin, which would hold his body was also ready. The pharaoh's mummy was carefully prepared, as befitted a great and beloved king. After seventy days, with solemn ceremony, Tuthmosis was laid in a tomb filled with all the choice food and drink, games and furniture, clothing and jewelry, and the little clay servant figures, called shawabtis (shah-WAHB-tees), that he could possibly need in the afterlife.

Following her father's death, Hatshepsut married her half brother, and the young man was crowned Pharaoh Tuthmosis II. Hatshepsut may have been only about twelve years old. As queen, she received a variety of new titles. Her favorite was God's Wife. Tuthmosis II and Hatshepsut had one child, a daughter named Neferure (neh-feh-ROO-ray).

The reign of Tuthmosis II was unremarkable. It was also brief, for he was a sickly young man. Within a few years of his coronation, Hatshepsut's husband had died.

With the death of Tuthmosis II, Egypt was left without a king to ensure that the many gods would look kindly upon the fragile desert land. *Maat* was a delicate thing, and without a pharaoh to tend to its preservation, it was in danger of collapsing.

Although Hatshepsut had been Tuthmosis II's Great Wife, he'd had other wives in his harem, including one named Isis. Isis had borne the pharaoh a baby boy, who was also named Tuthmosis. Since Isis was not royal, neither was her baby. But like his father, he could grow up to be pharaoh if he married a princess of the royal blood: his half sister, Neferure.

Until Tuthmosis III was mature enough to be crowned pharaoh what Egypt needed was a regent, an adult who could take control of the country. The regent would have to be someone familiar with palace life and protocol. He would need to conduct himself with the proper authority around the royal advisors. He should be prepared to wield power if it became necessary, and he should feel comfortable around visiting dignitaries from other lands. He needed to know his place among the priests of the various gods.

It was a job Hatshepsut, perhaps just fifteen years old, had been training for since her earliest days by her father's side. Women had acted as regents for infants at other times in Egypt's history, and the gods had not frowned upon them.

So until Tuthmosis III was ready to be crowned as pharaoh, the acting ruler of Egypt would be his aunt, the royal widow of the king, Hatshepsut.

"HIS SON STOOD IN HIS PLACE AS KING OF THE TWO LANDS, HAVING BECOME RULER UPON THE THRONE OF THE ONE WHO BEGAT HIM. HIS SISTER THE DIVINE CONSORT, HATSHEPSUT, SETTLED THE AFFAIRS OF THE TWO LANDS BY REASON OF HER PLANS. EGYPT WAS MADE TO LABOR WITH BOWED HEAD FOR HER."

At first, little Tuthmosis III was considered the pharaoh, with Hatshepsut just his second-in-command. But a small child could not be an effective ruler. As Hatshepsut settled into her role as regent, she gradually took on more and more of the royal decision-making. She appointed officials and advisors; dealt with the priests; appeared in public ceremonies first behind, then beside, and eventually in front of her nephew. Gradually, over seven years, her power and influence grew. In the end, Hatshepsut was ruling Egypt in all but name.

There is no reliable record of exactly when or how it happened, but at some point Hatshepsut took a bold and unprecedented step: She had herself crowned pharaoh with the large, heavy, red-and-white double crown of the two Egypts, north and south. Since all pharaohs took a throne name, a sort of symbolic name, upon their coronation, Hatshepsut chose Maatkare (maht-KAH-ray). *Maat,* that crucial cosmic order, was important to Hatshepsut. Egypt required a strong pharaoh to ensure *maat.* Hatshepsut could be that pharaoh—even if she did happen to be a woman.

"TO LOOK UPON HER WAS MORE BEAUTIFUL THAN ANYTHING."

A few women had tried to rule Egypt before, but never with such a valid claim to the throne or at such a time of peace and prosperity. When Queens Nitocris and Sobekneferu had come to the throne in earlier dynasties, Egypt had been suffering from political problems, and there had been no male heirs. These women had not ruled long or well, and neither had had the audacity to proclaim herself pharaoh. Hatshepsut would be different.

There was no word in the language of ancient Egypt for a female ruler; a queen was simply the wife of a king. Hatshepsut had no choice: She had to call herself pharaoh, or king—a male title. She was concerned with preserving and continuing traditional order as much as possible, so to the people of Egypt she made herself look like a man in her role as pharaoh. In ceremonies, she wore a man's short kilt instead of a woman's long dress, much as she had as a child. Around her neck she wore a king's broad collar. She even fastened a false golden beard to her chin. When she wrote about herself as pharaoh, sometimes she referred to herself as he, other times as she. This would be very confusing for historians trying to uncover her identity thousands of years later.

Since Hatshepsut could not marry a queen, her daughter Neferure acted as God's

Wife in public rituals. It was good training for Neferure, who would in time be expected to marry her half brother, Tuthmosis III, and be his royal consort. But Hatshepsut never seems to have considered that her daughter could succeed her as pharaoh.

Hatshepsut might have had to look and act like a man in public, but she never gave up feminine pleasures. Archaeologists have uncovered bracelets and alabaster cosmetic pots with Hatshepsut's cartouche (kar-TOOSH), or hieroglyphic name symbol, inscribed on each. Both men and women in Egypt used cosmetics. They needed creams and oils to keep their skin and hair from drying out under the brutal desert sun. And the kohl, a kind of makeup made from powdered lead that people applied around their eyes, did more than make them attractive; it also helped block out the sun's glare. But Hatshepsut was especially particular about her appearance. One inscription describes her as "more beautiful than anything."

With the exception of one military campaign against Nubia, Hatshepsut's reign was peaceful. Instead of expanding Egypt's borders through war and conquest, Hatshepsut built monuments within her country to proclaim its power. Her masterpiece was the magnificent temple at the site known today as Deir el-Bahri. The temple was dedicated to Amen, the god who was supposed to be the divine father of every pharaoh, the god to whom Hatshepsut felt she owed her good fortune. The temple at Deir el-Bahri was also to be Hatshepsut's own mortuary temple. The building is set into the side of a mountain and rises gracefully in three beautifully proportioned tiers, each supported by columns like those to be seen centuries later in Greek temples. Its design was far ahead of its time. Hatshepsut called it Djeser-Djeseru (JEH-sir jeh-SEH-roo)—"Holy of Holies."

On the walls of this temple, Hatshepsut had artists carve and paint her biography. According to the story told on the walls of Djeser-Djeseru, she had been chosen as pharaoh by the gods themselves, even before her birth. Perhaps, even after years on the throne, she still felt a need to justify a woman's right to rule. The gods in the pictures on the temple walls do not seem to care whether Hatshepsut is a man or a woman—in fact, some of the paintings show her as a boy.

"I WAS STATIONED AT THE 'STATION OF THE KING.'"

While Hatshepsut took care of the business of ruling Egypt, her nephew, Tuthmosis III, was being educated to reign as the next pharaoh. Traditionally, this involved periods of training as both a soldier and a priest. Tuthmosis III spent his religious service in the temple of the god Amen. But Tuthmosis never forgot that it was his birthright to become ruler of Egypt. Just as Hatshepsut said that the gods themselves had chosen her as king, Tuthmosis III had his own story to prove his divine claim to the throne.

On certain feast days, a procession of priests carried a statue of Amen, housed in an elaborate model boat, through the columned aisles of the temple at Karnak. On one of these holidays, Tuthmosis was standing in the temple among his fellow priests. Suddenly, the procession veered from its usual course—and the statue of Amen came to a stop in front of Tuthmosis. The young man was then led through the temple to the "Station of the King," the place where the pharaoh normally stood during a ceremony. It seemed that the god Amen had chosen Tuthmosis to be king.

But it would be years before this prophecy was fulfilled.

"I HAVE MADE FOR HIM A PUNT IN HIS GARDEN."

Perfumes played an important part in Egypt's ceremonies, and one of the rarest and finest was myrrh (MUHR). Myrrh was made from the resin of a tree that grew, not in Egypt, but in the faraway land of Punt. Historians today are not sure just where Punt was, but it was probably somewhere in southern Africa, perhaps Somalia or Ethiopia. For many generations, however, no Egyptian had made the long and hazardous sea journey to the land of Punt.

Nine years into her reign, Hatshepsut sent out an expedition to travel to Punt. Her purpose was not war or conquest, but trade and exploration. After two long years with no word from the travelers, their ships finally returned to Thebes laden with wonders. There were perfumes and gold; ivory and ebony; live panthers, leopards, and cheetahs (probably imported from India); an amazing giraffe; clever monkeys and baboons; even men and women from that strange land to the south. But the finest treasure of all was thirty-one live myrrh trees, their roots bound in balls of soil from Punt. The trees were planted in a fragrant avenue in Djeser-Djeseru. The travelers also told fabulous stories about the people of Punt, who lived in grass huts on stilts, and whose queen, riding about on a donkey, was grotesquely fat—a curious trait to the traditionally slender Egyptians.

For Hatshepsut, the expedition to Punt was one of the highlights of her reign. It was the sort of accomplishment she wanted memorialized forever in her mortuary temple. She had her artists record a detailed account of the journey on the interior walls of Djeser-Djeseru which remains to this day.

"I WAS ONE WHOSE STEPS WERE KNOWN IN THE PALACE; A REAL CONFIDANT[E] OF THE KING, HIS BELOVED: OVERSEER OF THE GARDEN OF AMON, SEN[EN]MUT."

All rulers need their trusted advisors, and Hatshepsut's favorite was Senenmut (SEN-en-moot). Although Senenmut came from a humble family, he was one of the few people in Egypt at the time (only about five percent) who had learned to read and write. Since he was bright, ambitious, and skillful, he quickly advanced as a scribe. Senenmut soon attracted the attention of the pharaoh, and Hatshepsut appointed him as her daughter's tutor. She gradually gave him more and more challenging assignments, including supervision of her various building projects. The unusual design of Djeser-Djeseru itself may have been Senenmut's idea.

As his attachment to Hatshepsut increased, Senenmut grew wealthy as well as powerful. His father, who had died before Senenmut's rise into the royal circle, had been buried very simply. But when his mother died, his style of living was quite different. Senenmut was able to buy two elaborately painted coffins for his parents and had his father's body moved to a fine new tomb. Then, in a bold move, he ordered a rich sarcophagus—something only royalty usually enjoyed—for himself. He also began excavating a tomb, complete with a ceiling painted with spectacular diagrams of the constellations, just beneath Djeser-Djeseru. As if this wasn't audacious enough, Senenmut also had small sketches of himself, accompanied by prayers, carved inside the doors to some of the temple's chapels. Today, some historians think that Senenmut fell from Hatshepsut's favor when she learned what he was doing around her temple. Senenmut's rich sarcophagus and tomb were never occupied, his mummy has never been found, and his name disappears from the records suddenly between the sixteenth and nineteenth years of Hatshepsut's reign.

But others believe that Hatshepsut knew and approved of her advisor's private projects, and that his unoccupied tomb may simply mean that he died far from Thebes, traveling on one of his many assignments. Some people, in fact, think that Senenmut may have been more than Hatshepsut's advisor. It seems Senenmut never married, unusual in ancient Egypt; so rumors of romance inevitably sprang up, linking Senenmut to the pharaoh herself. Archaeologists have discovered an amethyst bead with both their names carved onto the tiny bit of stone. It is intriguing to wonder whether the rumors about the pharaoh and her friend and advisor were true.

"THEIR RAYS FLOOD THE TWO LANDS WHEN THE SUN RISES BETWEEN THEM, AS HE DAWNS IN THE HORIZON OF HEAVEN."

After Hatshepsut had been on the throne for fifteen years, she declared a jubilee, a year of special celebration. Most pharaohs held a jubilee in the thirtieth year of their reign; maybe Hatshepsut felt she had accomplished enough in half that time to deserve a celebration. Or perhaps she was celebrating her thirtieth birthday. To mark the event, she ordered two tall, needle-shaped stone monuments, called obelisks (AH-beh-lisks), to be built and erected in her father's temple at Karnak. In ancient Egypt, obelisks honored Re, the sun god, for they represented the first rays of sunlight ever to strike the earth. One of Hatshepsut's obelisks still stands. More than ninety-seven feet high, it remains the tallest ancient monument in Egypt.

The construction of these obelisks in just seven months was a massive feat of engineering. The monuments were hewn whole from granite in a quarry many miles from Thebes. One of the huge blocks cracked as it was being shaped, and the workmen had to start all over again on a new piece of stone. The completed obelisks, each weighing one thousand pounds, were then loaded onto barges. It took twenty-seven boats rowed by eight-hundred-and-fifty strong men to guide the barges down the Nile to Karnak. The problems were far from over when the immense stone monuments arrived at their destination. Since the obelisks were taller than the temple hall at Karnak, the roof had to be removed to fit them in.

Hatshepsut wanted to coat the two obelisks in gold from top to bottom, but this proved too costly, even for the pharaoh. So she finally settled for painting just their tips with electrum, a mixture of silver and gold. On the bases of the obelisks, Hatshepsut placed inscriptions praising the gods—and herself.

"O MY MOTHER NUT, STRETCH THYSELF OVER ME, THAT THOU MAYEST PLACE ME AMONG THE STARS IMPERISHABLE THAT ARE IN THEE, AND THAT I MAY NOT DIE."

Ancient Egyptians were very practical regarding their own deaths, and they prepared for their burial throughout their lives. At different stages in her life—as queen, and then as pharaoh—Hatshepsut had ordered craftsmen to fashion several fine sarcophagi for her. After becoming pharaoh, she selected her burial place in the Valley of the Kings, not far from her father's tomb. In fact, she planned to have his mummy moved to her own tomb, probably to keep it safe from grave robbers. Ancient Egyptians held strong beliefs about an afterlife, so it was a terrible sacrilege to disturb a mummy. But for some poor or greedy people, the gold included in a wealthy burial was hard to resist. Grave robbers dug their way through piles of rubble meant to hide the entrances to the tombs. They pulled the heavy stone lids from sarcophagi, split open the wooden coffins inside, and unwrapped the linen strips from mummies, looking for gold rings, necklaces, and bracelets. Hatshepsut hoped the tomb intended for herself and her father was well hidden from grave robbers. Its entrance was inconspicuous among the sheer cliffs of the Valley of the Kings, and reaching the burial chamber itself involved a long and winding walk down steep, unlit steps and along dark corridors curving through the limestone bowels of the desert hills.

At last, in early February in the twenty-second year of her reign, Hatshepsut died. There have been rumors that she died under suspicious circumstances, perhaps even murdered by Tuthmosis III. But Hatshepsut was no longer young by ancient Egyptian standards; she was probably in her forties. She had reigned for a very long time without any sign of rebellion from her nephew. Impatient as he must have been to become pharaoh, it seems unlikely that Tuthmosis III would have brought about Hatshepsut's death after so many peaceful years.

"HE [DID] MORE THAN ANY KING
WHO HAS BEEN SINCE THE BEGINNING."

Following Hatshepsut's death, Tuthmosis III was finally crowned pharaoh. He would enjoy more than thirty conquest-filled years as king. Perhaps he did marry Hatshepsut's daughter, Neferure, although there is no clear evidence of it. Like Senenmut's, Neferure's name disappears in the course of Hatshepsut's long reign. This could mean that she died young; it could also simply mean that she did nothing worth noting.

Some time after he assumed the double crown, Tuthmosis III embarked upon a fierce attempt to erase all evidence of Hatshepsut's reign from the face of Egypt. He changed the royal records to make it look as if he had succeeded his father directly, without another pharaoh—and certainly not a female pharaoh—between them. He ordered countless statues of Hatshepsut to be smashed, and had stonecutters chip away her face from wall carvings. Hatshepsut's name was chiseled out of inscriptions, and Tuthmosis's name was substituted. The myrrh trees in Djeser-Djeseru were left unwatered and untended—and were perhaps even burned. A wall was built in the temple at Karnak to try to hide Hatshepsut's towering obelisks.

Besides rewriting history in his own favor, Tuthmosis III may also have been trying to bring about a "second death" for Hatshepsut. If every trace of a person's name and likeness could be obliterated, ancient Egyptians believed that the person's soul, or *ka,* would cease to exist in the afterlife as well. But for some reason, Tuthmosis III was not as thorough as that. A few of Hatshepsut's royal cartouches and inscriptions remained in obscure places; a few statues were still identifiable, even if they were in pieces.

Thousands of years later, archaeologists would have a difficult job trying to figure out who Hatshepsut had been—difficult, but not impossible.

"HER ANNALS ARE MYRIADS OF YEARS."

Although Tuthmosis III had managed to remove Hatshepsut's name from most of the official lists of kings, one ancient record survived that indicated there was a pharaoh around 1470 B.C. who was not a Tuthmosis—who was, in fact, a woman. The name, however, was badly garbled. During the 1800s, Jean-François Champollion, who would decode the writing on the Rosetta Stone and pave the way for translation of ancient documents, found and deciphered some cartouches of a king named Maatkare Hatshepsut. But he was confused. Sometimes the references to the pharaoh were masculine, sometimes feminine. Champollion incorrectly believed that this pharaoh was a man. But archaeologists were gradually becoming more aware of Hatshepsut's contradictory identity.

In the early 1900s, Howard Carter, famous for discovering the tomb of Pharaoh Tutankhamen, found the burial chamber intended for Hatshepsut. Inside were two sarcophagi, one for Hatshepsut, the other for Tuthmosis I. Carter also found fragments of a canopic chest marked with Hatshepsut's name. The chest would have contained the jars used to hold the internal organs removed during mummification. Unfortunately, there was no mummy anywhere in the tomb.

In fact, no mummy that can definitely be identified as Hatshepsut's has ever been found. Archaeologists did discover a number of royal mummies crammed into a single chamber near Deir el-Bahri, apparently hidden there to keep them safe from grave robbers. Many were in mismarked coffins, and some remain unidentified. One of them may be Hatshepsut. Some people, however, believe that Hatshepsut's mummy will never be found, because it does not exist: If Tuthmosis III was so unhappy about succeeding a female pharaoh that he destroyed Hatshepsut's images, perhaps he did not bury his aunt with the ceremony due a king. Yet another possibility is that Hatshepsut, who loved clever

building projects, had her workmen construct one more burial chamber, a tomb that has remained secret for millennia, hidden from grave robbers as well as archaeologists.

In its excavations at Deir el-Bahri in the 1920s, a team from New York's Metropolitan Museum of Art uncovered an ancient rubbish pit. It was filled not with garbage, but with stone: pieces of huge statues, broken into small fragments and sometimes even burned. The project's director, Herbert Winlock, described the process of reassembling the bits: "Imagine nearly a hundred jigsaw puzzles, every one of them lacking some parts and most of them with little or next to nothing left, all mixed up together. Picture some of the pieces no bigger than the tip of your finger and others so heavy that it took a large derrick to move them. Then consider that the edges of these pieces were often so delicate that they crumbled away unless they were handled with the most delicate care—even when they weighed a ton or more." The "Hatshepsut Hole," as the archaeologists called the pit, was a rich source of information about a woman whose existence and importance had only recently come to light.

Some of the approximately two hundred statues which had once stood along the pathways and among the columns of Djeser-Djeseru were sphinxes: lions' bodies with human heads. Others depicted a pharaoh's head atop a mummylike body. Still others seemed to be more lifelike images of a king with feminine features, wearing the traditional male beard, collar, and kilt, as well as the ceremonial crowns of the pharaoh. And some were definitely statues of a woman. Every one of these was a representation of Hatshepsut, the mysterious female pharaoh barely mentioned in the most ancient histories. And each was mutilated in a similar fashion. The uraeus (yoo-RAY-us), the serpent-shaped symbol on the front of the king's crown, was always broken off. The statues' eyes were gouged out so, symbolically, Hatshepsut could not see; the noses were broken off so she could not breathe. In many cases, the archaeologists succeeded in piecing together nearly complete stone portraits of Hatshepsut for the first time in millennia.

The full story of Hatshepsut's life may never be known. Many facts were certainly

lost when the pharaoh's images, cartouches, and statues were destroyed during the reign of Tuthmosis III. But as archaeologists continue to study Djeser-Djeseru, the amazing tale told on its walls and the broken statues discarded in its precincts, more and more about Egypt's only successful female pharaoh is revealed. After thousands of years in obscurity, Hatshepsut is finally gaining her rightful place in history.

FOR MORE INFORMATION

A diamond (♦) indicates a good source for young readers

♦ ASHBY, RUTH, AND DEBORAH GORE OHRN, eds. *Herstory: Women Who Changed the World.* New York: Viking, 1995.

♦ CARTER, DOROTHY SHARP. *His Majesty, Queen Hatshepsut.* New York: J. B. Lippincott, 1987. A fictional version of the life of the pharaoh, for young adult readers.

COTTRELL, LEONARD. *Lady of the Two Lands: Five Queens of Ancient Egypt.* Indianapolis: Bobbs-Merrill, 1967.

♦ "Egypt's Great Queen." (*Video recording*) *New York: A&E Television Network/A&E Home Video, 1998.*

GREENBLATT, MIRIAM. *Hatshepsut and Ancient Egypt.* New York: Benchmark, 2000.

RAY, JOHN. "Hatshepsut, the Female Pharaoh." *History Today.* May 1994, pp. 23–29.

♦ SCIESZKA, JON. *Tut Tut.* New York: Viking, 1996. A humorous time-travel fantasy featuring Hatshepsut and Thutmose (Tuthmosis) III.

TYLDESLEY, JOYCE. *Hatchepsut: The Female Pharaoh.* New York: Viking, 1996.

WELLS, EVELYN. *Hatshepsut.* Garden City, N.Y.: Doubleday, 1969.

CREDITS

Inscriptions on pages 6, 8, 10, 14, 18, 20, 24, 26, 28, 30, 34, and 36 are from *Ancient Records of Egypt,* vol. 2, by James Henry Breasted (University of Chicago Press, 1906).

Inscription on page 32 is from "Tomb Prepared for Queen Hatshepsuit," by Howard Carter, in *Journal of Egyptian Archaeology,* vol. 4 (1917). Courtesy of the Committee of the Egypt Exploration Society.

Quotation on page 38 is from *Excavations at Deir el-Bahri* by Herbert E. Winlock (Macmillan, 1942).

PLACES TO LOOK FOR HATSHEPSUT

You don't have to go to Egypt to find images of Hatshepsut. The Metropolitan Museum of Art in New York City has a room devoted to the statues of Hatshepsut that were discovered in fragments and pieced back together. In a nearby gallery are assorted artifacts including sketches of Senenmut's face, a reconstruction of his sarcophagus, and fragments of the "astronomical" ceiling paintings from his tomb. One of the sarcophagi found in Hatshepsut's tomb—the one intended for her father—is on exhibit at Boston's Museum of Fine Arts. Her successor's handiwork is easy to find, too. Two obelisks stand, one on the banks of the River Thames in London, England, and the other in Central Park in New York City, just behind the Metropolitan Museum. These obelisks were built by Tuthmosis III—though in Egypt, not where they stand today!